NATIVE PEOPLES OF NORTH AMERICA

Native Peoples of THE SUBARCTIC

By Amy Hayes

Gareth Stevens
PUBLISHING

Please visit our website, www.garethstevens.com. For a free color catalog of all our high-quality books, call toll free 1-800-542-2595 or fax 1-877-542-2596.

Cataloging-in-Publication Data

Names: Hayes, Amy.
Title: Native peoples of the subarctic / Amy Hayes.
Description: New York : Gareth Stevens Publishing, 2017. | Series: Native peoples of North America| Includes index.
Identifiers: ISBN 9781482448368 (pbk.) | ISBN 9781482448214 (library bound) | ISBN 9781482447675 (6 pack)
Subjects: LCSH: Indians of North America–Canada, Northern –Juvenile literature. | Indians of North America–Alaska–Juvenile literature.
Classification: LCC E78.C2 H39 2017 | DDC 971.9'01–dc23

First Edition

Published in 2017 by
Gareth Stevens Publishing
111 East 14th Street, Suite 349
New York, NY 10003

Designer: Samantha DeMartin
Editor: Kristen Nelson

Photo credits: Series Art AlexTanya/Shutterstock.com; cover, p. 1 Hulton Archive/Hulton Archive/Getty Images; p. 5 (main) Bjoern Alberts/Shutterstock.com; p. 5 (map) AlexCovarrubias/Wikimedia Commons; p. 7 Grigorly Pil/Shutterstock.com; pp. 9, 19 UniversalImagesGroup/Universal Images Group/Getty Images; p. 11 courtesy of the Library of Congress; p. 13 Underwood Archives/Archive Photos/Getty Images; p. 15 Print Collector/Hulton Archive/Getty Images; p. 17 Doug Wilson/The LIFE Images Collection/Getty Images; p. 21 (main) John Greim/LightRocket/Getty Images; p. 21 (inset) Sergey Krasnoshchokov/Shutterstock.com; p. 23 David Prichard/First Light/Getty Images; p. 25 Stock Montage/Archive Photos/Getty Images; p. 27 Raymond K. Gehman/National Geographic/Getty Images; p. 29 (paper) caesart/Shutterstock.com; p. 29 (background) photosoft/Shutterstock.com.

Printed in the United States of America

CPSIA compliance information: Batch #CS16GS: For further information contact Gareth Stevens, New York, New York at 1-800-542-2595.

CONTENTS

Words in the glossary appear in **bold** type the first time they are used in the text.

Who Were the Subarctic PEOPLE?

You may know about the Inuit who lived in the cold **region** of the Arctic and the Algonquin who lived around the Great Lakes. But many native peoples also lived in the central part of Canada and throughout the huge **wilderness** that's now Alaska! This region is called the Subarctic.

The native peoples of the Subarctic moved from place to place, **developing** their own special **cultures**. Even so, these native groups shared traditions, or ways of life.

The Subarctic region covers much of what is the US state of Alaska and several of Canada's **provinces** today.

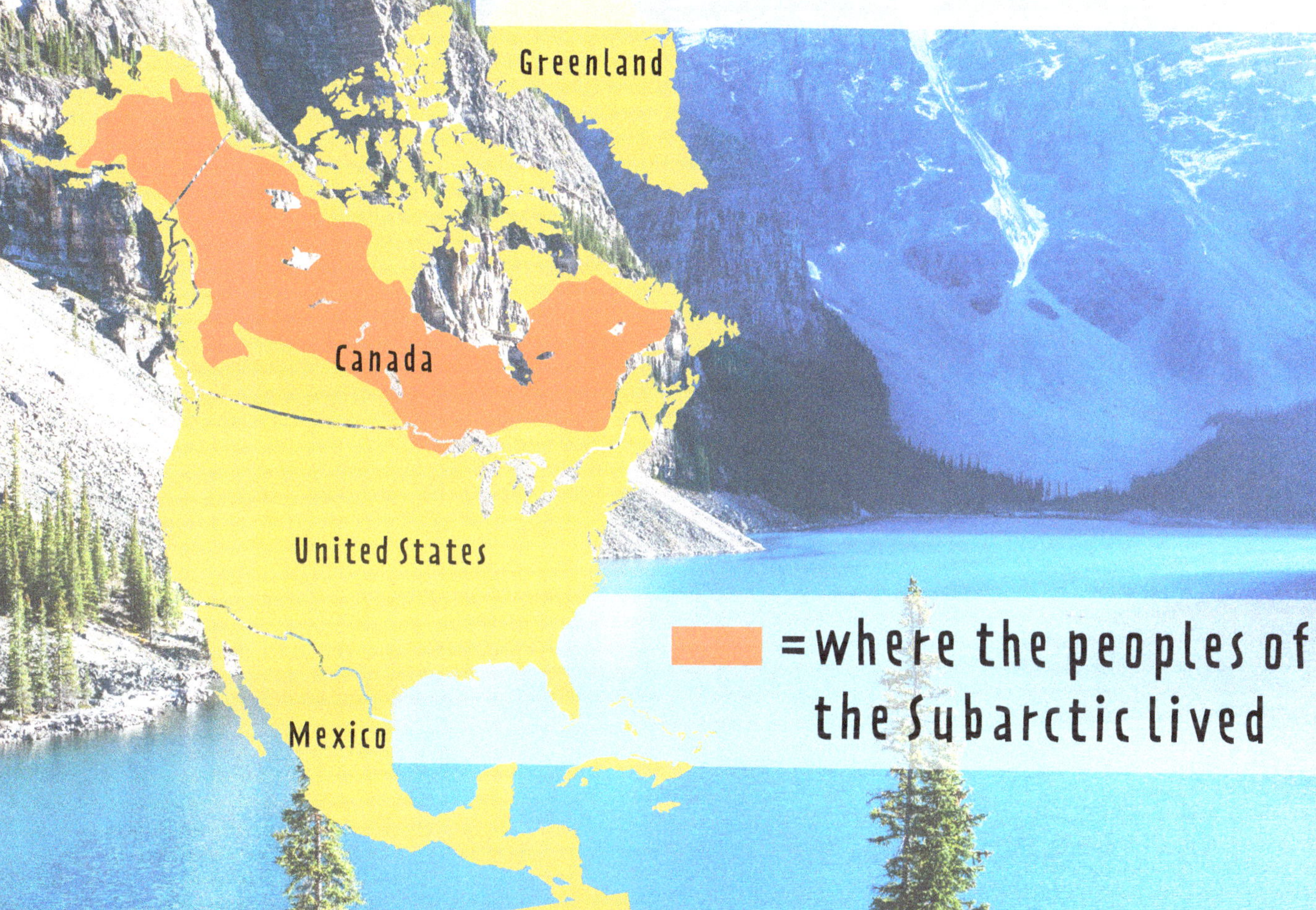

TELL ME MORE

The native peoples of Canada are called the First Nations.

The Cold NORTH

Because of the **climate**, the Subarctic has never been very populated. The weather is some of the coldest in the world, and the winters are long. Daylight can last nearly 24 hours in summer, and in winter, the world is wrapped in darkness.

This land is taiga (TY-guh), a **biome** that's covered in forest. Among the snow and the thick woods, the native Alaskans and the First Nations peoples of Canada braved the quickly changing weather and made their home.

The taiga is huge, taking up most of Canada and Alaska. There were many peoples who lived here long before the Europeans came.

Food from the HUNT

Cold winters, lack of sunlight, and short summers meant that growing crops wasn't a possibility for the people who lived in the Subarctic. Instead, groups such as the Dane-zaa, Ojibwe, and Cree were **nomadic**. They moved from place to place in search of food.

These northern groups became skilled hunters, eating musk ox, elk, water birds, and even moose. People also used the lakes and ocean as sources of food. Ice fishing was a popular way to catch dinner.

TELL ME MORE

The First Nations peoples and native Alaskans also gathered berries, dandelions, moss, and other plants. They prepared pemmican, too, which was made with berries, meat, and fat. It could keep for years!

Elk can be 5 feet (1.5 m) tall at the shoulder and can weigh up to 1,100 pounds (499 kg)! Can you imagine trying to hunt one for dinner?

Following the HERD

The people of the Subarctic went where the food was, and this changed throughout the year. Groups would follow animals through the seasons, catching ducks and geese by the lakes and bays in the fall. Then, they would head inland to hunt caribou, members of the deer family, in early winter.

Where the groups moved depended on where they lived and what food they were looking for. For example, the Deg Xinag, who lived in modern Alaska, settled by lakes in the spring to fish.

TELL ME MORE

The Deg Xinag also built **permanent** villages.

In the summer, groups of Ojibwe would gather at good places to fish.

Ojibwe Canoes and SNOWSHOES

Hunting herds required packing light and easy traveling. Walking through many feet of snow could be pretty hard, however. Subarctic peoples such as the Ojibwe built snowshoes with wood frames. They allowed people to walk on the heavy snow without sinking into it. They also used *nobugidabans*, which were long wooden sleds.

Many groups built canoes for travel, but the Ojibwe were known for their skill. The Ojibwe canoes were built with birch bark, commonly gathered from one tree.

TELL ME MORE

Ojibwe canoes could be 36 feet (11 m) long and carry 6,000 pounds (2,720 kg), but were light enough when empty to be carried by only four men.

Today, the Ojibwe still make birch bark canoes. They're useful and beautiful works of art.

Hunting Units of the DENESULINÉ

Most Subarctic peoples lived and moved with just their family. They sometimes joined other families to make groups of 20 to 30 people. The Denesuliné, who lived in what's now northern Saskatchewan, called these groups hunting units. They're also often called bands.

Hunting units worked together to hunt bigger animals such as moose and elk. The Denesuliné were often headed by an *asegolia*, or **medicine man**. But on the hunt, a headman would be chosen because of his hunting knowledge.

The native peoples of the Subarctic relied on their families and bands. They believed everyone needed to work for the good of the group.

The Gwich'in on the HUNT

The Gwich'in, or Kutchin, were a native group of the Subarctic who lived around the Yukon and the Peel Rivers in Alaska and Yukon Territory. The Gwich'in were skilled hunters.

To hunt game, they used bows, arrows, and long, sharpened sticks called spears. The bows were made from birch wood and willow. In spring and summer, they would drive caribou into nearby lakes or rivers. It was easier for the hunters to spear the animals while they were in the water. The Gwich'in also used spears and nets to catch fish.

Today, about 6,000 Gwich'in live in the Northwest Territories, Yukon Territory, and Alaska.

TELL ME MORE

Another way the Gwich'in caught dinner was with deadfalls, or traps made by digging a pit and covering it with leaves and grass. Animals would fall in and be unable to escape.

The Wigwam and the TEPEE

Most of the native people of the Subarctic traveled from place to place, but they often settled in one place for a season.

The Cree handled this by building two types of houses. When they were on the move, the Cree would live in tepees made out of bison hide. These were easy to move across the plains, especially with a team of dogs to carry the load. However, when they settled in a forest for a season, the Cree would build wigwams.

TELL ME MORE

Wigwams were **dome**-shaped houses made from young trees covered in birch bark. They could survive harsh weather, and some were quite large.

To the Cree, home could be many places in the Subarctic.

The Athabascan Keep WARM

Warm clothing was important to survival in the taiga. The Athabascan, a wide-ranging group of people who spoke similar languages, created beautiful clothing from the hides of animals. They would keep the fur of the animal on the hide, and in cold weather turned the fur inward, which kept them warm.

Both men and women wore pants, soft shoes called moccasins, long coats, and fur hoods. Clothing was mostly made from the hides of caribou.

Though the heavy coats and shoes kept them dry and warm, the Athabascans also wore lighter underclothes. These were made from the hides of the snowshoe hare.

TELL ME MORE

Those who spoke Athabascan languages were part of one big grouping of Subarctic peoples often called the Dene, which means "people."

caribou

Fishing with the DOGRIB

The Dogrib were one smaller group within the Dene. "Dogrib" is an English shortening of the name they called themselves, Tlicho Doné, which means "dog rib people." It comes from a Dogrib story about a hero who had once been a dog.

The Dogrib lived in the Northwest Territories of Canada between two lakes. Because the Dogrib lived near these lakes and other waterways, fishing was a big part of Dogrib culture. They used nets, hooks, and even made fishing poles.

The Northwest Territories where the Dogrib lived are one of the northernmost parts of Canada. Many people of this native group still live there today!

A Nation of BEAVERS

The Dane-zaa, or Tsattine, were a group of Athabascan people whose name means "those who live among the beavers." Sometimes called the Beavers, the Dane-zaa originally lived in Alberta and Saskatchewan. They moved as far as the Rocky Mountains in search of food and to escape fighting with the Cree.

When Beaver boys were young teenagers, they went on journeys called vision quests. They didn't eat or sleep much. But when they did sleep, a dream of an animal spirit was supposed to come to them.

The Beaver people believed in spirits that guarded them.

The SLAVEY

The Slavey lived in the very north of Alberta and were also known as the Acha'otinne. Like many of the Subartic peoples, they lived in family bands, moving from place to place. Men in the family hunted animals, while women took care of the household, caught small game, collected berries, and made clothing.

A commonly peaceful people, the Slavey were known for being wonderful storytellers. They were also known by surrounding people to be powerful **sorcerers** who could perform magic.

Like many Subarctic peoples, the Slavey's way of life was greatly affected by Europeans coming to North America. Many of their traditions survive today across Canada and Alaska, though.

TELL ME MORE

Shamans were spiritual leaders and healers of the Slavey. These medicine men used roots, animal parts, and plants in magical cures.

Fur Trade and TODAY

Beginning in the 1500s, the fur trade with Europeans changed how the native groups of the Subarctic moved around, as many wanted to trade even more. However, European settlement also harmed native ways of life. Many native peoples died of European illnesses.

For many years, the native peoples of the Subarctic were treated poorly. Then, in 1999, the Canadian government created Nunavut, a region for native peoples to live in. A First Nations government headed it, too. Their cultures can now live on more easily.

The native groups of the Subarctic shared many ways of life that allowed them to survive the cold of the Subarctic region.

GUIDE TO SURVIVING THE SUBARCTIC

HUNT caribou, moose, and musk ox

TRAVEL by canoe

MAKE snowshoes

FISH in the many waterways

MAKE clothing from animal hide

BUILD wigwams and tepees

MOVE with the seasons

WORK together

GLOSSARY

biome: a natural community of plants and animals, such as a forest or desert

climate: the average weather conditions of a place over a period of time

culture: the beliefs and ways of life of a group of people

develop: to grow and change

dome: a rounded roof

medicine man: someone who acted as a healer and leader in a band

nomadic: having to do with people who move from place to place

permanent: meant to last a long time

province: an area of a country

region: a large area of land that has features that make it different from nearby areas of land

sorcerer: someone who does magic

wilderness: a piece of unoccupied land left to grow wild

For More INFORMATION

Books

Doak, Robin S. *Subarctic Peoples.* Chicago, IL: Heinemann Library, 2012.

Kuiper, Kathleen. *Indigenous Peoples of the Arctic, Subarctic, and Northwest Coast.* New York, NY: Rosen Educational Services, LLC, 2012.

Websites

National Museum of the American Indian

nmai.si.edu/

You can explore the museum's exhibits on their website!

Sub-Arctic Indians

warpaths2peacepipes.com/native-american-indians/sub-arctic-indians.htm

Discover facts about the culture of the Subarctic here.

Subarctic People

firstpeoplesofcanada.com/fp_groups/fp_subarctic1.html

Read more about the First Nations of Canada's Subarctic.

Publisher's note to educators and parents: Our editors have carefully reviewed these websites to ensure that they are suitable for students. Many websites change frequently, however, and we cannot guarantee that a site's future contents will continue to meet our high standards of quality and educational value. Be advised that students should be closely supervised whenever they access the Internet.

INDEX